LIZ STARIN
SPLASHDANCE

FARRAR STRAUS GIROUX • **New York**

For Tobi and Eric Starin,
who love justice and swimming

Farrar Straus Giroux Books for Young Readers
175 Fifth Avenue, New York 10010

Copyright © 2016 by Liz Starin
Color separations by Bright Arts (H.K.) Ltd.
Printed in the United States of America by
Phoenix Color, Hagerstown, Maryland
First edition, 2016
3 5 7 9 10 8 6 4 2

mackids.com

Library of Congress Cataloging-in-Publication Data
Names: Starin, Liz.
Title: Splashdance / Liz Starin.
Description: New York : Farrar Straus Giroux, 2016. | Summary: "Ursula, a bear, and Ricardo, a human,
   are preparing for the water ballet competition. But a new regulation at the community pool—no
   bears—leaves Ursula cut from the contest. Luckily, she encounters a group of undaunted animal
   swimmers at a local pond, and Ursula and her new team figure out a way to participate in the
   competition and make sure everyone is welcome at the pool once and for all"—Provided by publisher.
Identifiers: LCCN 2015039452 | ISBN 9780374300982 (hardback)
Subjects: CYAC: Bears—Fiction. | Swimming—Fiction. | Teamwork
   (Sports)—Fiction. | Toleration—Fiction. | BISAC: JUVENILE FICTION /
   Animals / Bears. | JUVENILE FICTION / Sports & Recreation / Water Sports.
Classification: LCC PZ7.S2502 Sp 2016 | DDC [E]—dc23
LC record available at http://lccn.loc.gov/2015039452

Our books may be purchased in bulk for promotional, educational, or business use.
Please contact your local bookseller or the Macmillan Corporate and Premium Sales Department
at (800) 221-7945 ext. 5442 or by e-mail at MacmillanSpecialMarkets@macmillan.com.

REALLY
REALLY DEEP

Ursula and Ricardo were taking a swim.

They were practicing their moves for the upcoming water ballet championship.

The prize was one million dollars.

So they trained and trained.

"Man, I really want to win," said Ursula.
"We can do it," said Ricardo. "We're a team!"

But one morning, they got a terrible surprise.

"New policy," said the lifeguard. "Bears are too hairy."

"But I'm a very clean bear," said Ursula. "I comb twice a day!"

"Tough noogies," said the lifeguard.

"What about that guy?" said Ricardo.

"SCRAM," said the lifeguard.

"Don't worry," whispered Ursula. "I know what to do."

The next day, Ursula was ready for practice. So was Ricardo. So was . . . Hortense.

"Ursula, meet my new partner," said Ricardo.

"WHAT?!" gasped Ursula.

Ursula went home and cried for a week.

Sometimes she slunk down to the neighborhood pond. She did her fanciest moves, all alone.

DOUBLE BACK ALBATROSS

MARY LOU BOOGALOO

HALF TWIST CHANTERELLE

Ursula was in a big, big funk.

One gloomy day, the pond was already occupied.

"It figures," said Ursula. Then she looked again.

"Wow, great moves!" said Ursula.

"Thanks!" said a bear. "We were up for the championship, but now we're stuck in this pond. I'm Ralph."

"Your team didn't ditch you?" Ursula asked.

"Of course not. We're a team!" Ralph said.

"Hmm, I think I have an idea,"
said Ursula. "May I join you?"

Ursula and her new teammates worked hard to prepare.

Soon the big day arrived, and at the crowded pool
entrance, there were no bears in sight.

It was a day of fierce competition.

Ricardo and Hortense performed
a graceful duet.

"Okay, ladies and gerbils," said the judge. "Let's thank all the swimmers before we announce the winners of—"

"READY,"

boomed a chorus of voices.

"SET."

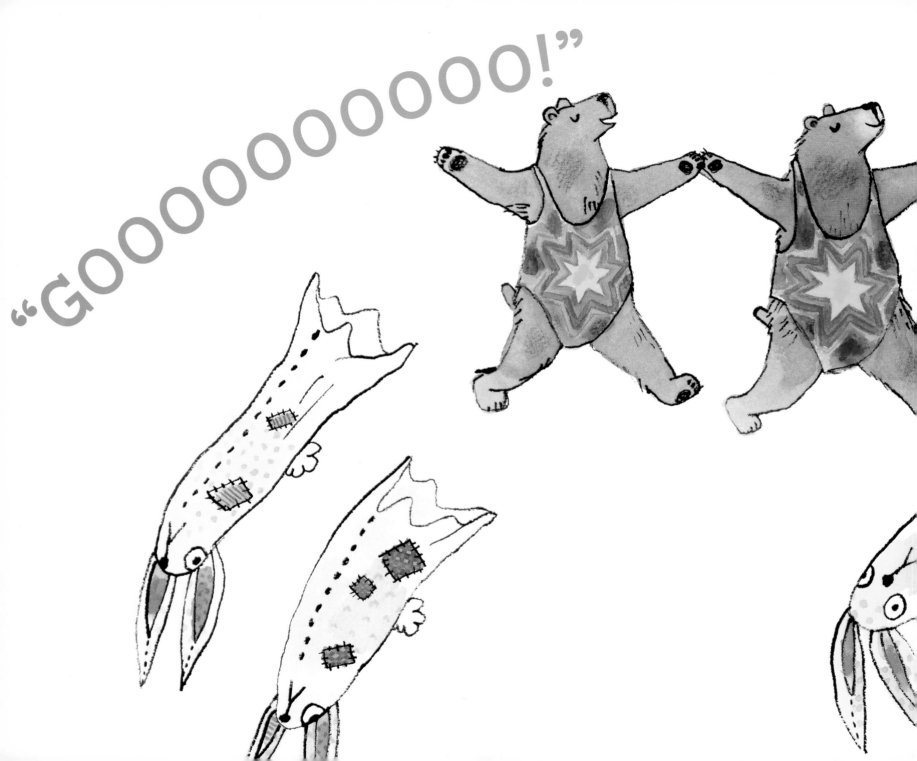

The crowd exploded!

Ursula's team staged a complicated routine,
with Ursula's triple banana flip as the finale.

They bowed. Then they marched out.

"Well," said the judge, "please help me
congratulate our *winners*, Ricardo and Hortense!"
But the audience had other ideas.

WATER BALLET
CHAMPIONSHIPS (NO BEARS)

Meanwhile, Ursula was steamed.
"We were so much better than those
turkeys!" she said. "Why didn't we win?"
"Look," said Ralph. "We did."

Ursula and Ralph—and Hector and Lucy and Wilma
and Bo—were taking a swim.

They were practicing their moves for the upcoming
water ballet championship. The prize was one million
dollars.

So they trained and trained.